AMBUSHED!

Bill pulled open the office door and stepped inside. He thought it odd that the lamp on the desk was without its shade. The light was so bright that he had to squint against its glare. In a moment his eyes focused to the glare and what he first saw was the sheriff, lying facedown on the floor, hands and arms laced behind him with a piece of rope and a blue bandanna tied about his mouth.

His glance moved to the back of the room. Ray Mankey was standing with his back to the jail door, his hands raised to the level of his shoulders, the holsters at his thighs empty.

Suddenly, to Bill's left, Tom Bostwick's deep voice intoned: "Careful, Brand! Don't move!"

Bill turned his head to see the rancher, standing less than four feet away, between the door and the window. He held a double-barreled Greener leveled squarely at Bill's waist....

PETER DAWSON

FORGOTT
DESTINY

LEISURE BOOKS NE

TABLE OF CONTENTS

Brand of Luck

Jonathan Glidden, who wrote as Peter Dawson, completed this story in October, 1940. It was sold to *Complete Western Book Magazine* on November 3, 1940. Glidden's title for the story was "An Outcast Deputy's Brand of Luck," and he was paid $108.00 for it. The editor changed the title to "Land-Grabber, I'll Be Back with Guns" for publication in *Complete Western Book Magazine* (3/41). The story was reprinted more than a decade later in *Complete Western Book Magazine* (9/54) as "I'll Be Back, Landhog!" For the story's first book appearance the author's original title has been somewhat shortened.

I

The cabin had lost its air of disuse. New yellow pine shakes unevenly splotched the gray, tinder-dry slant of its roof, and along its sides showed an occasional fresh slab with the bark still brown and yellow. The wagon shed out back gave evidence of the same neat hand, while the lean-to near the corral was new and staunchly built. The green carpet of the valley climbed the knoll and made a pleasing yard out front, a yard now orderly where three months ago brush and rusty tin cans had completed the lay-out's desolate appearance.

Hugh Conner, his tall, flat frame propped indolently against one corner of his cabin, gazed unsmilingly at the two men standing near their ground-haltered ponies thirty feet out in the yard, and said tonelessly: "No one wanted it, so I'm here."

"Someone wants it now," the tallest of the pair growled, his belligerence obvious. He was thin almost to gauntness, and on the upper left-hand pocket of the vest beneath his canvas windbreaker showed a sheriff's five-pointed star. His light-colored blue eyes were red-rimmed and dull from too much whisky. Sheriff Mace Dow didn't command the respect due his badge.

"Who wants it?"

"I've already filed on it," answered Mace Dow's companion. "One of my crew will be up here next week. He's homesteading in my name."

"Why didn't you come to me before you filed, Keyes?"

Wyatt Keyes lifted his thick shoulders in a careless shrug. "You're a squatter, Conner. I didn't think it necessary to consult you."

His sarcasm was biting, eloquent of the man's habitual arrogance. Looking at Keyes now, Hugh Conner wondered at the stubborn will that had brought the man so far in ten years. This last summer Keyes's Key-Bar had calmly bluffed George Baird's Chain Link, the biggest outfit in this country, and made Baird give over ten sections of choice summer graze high in the hills. A legal loophole had made it possible, and with the help of his sheriff—Mace Dow had two years ago been Key-Bar foreman—he'd made it stick. Now he was buying up this valley. Hugh hadn't been surprised at their call this afternoon, for he had heard of Keyes's visits to some of his neighbors above, but it galled him to have to give up something he had made from nothing and with his own hands. Every day for three months, since the time he had first came to this country, he had worked at his cabin and his